A JIGSAW JONES MYSTERY

# The Case of the Disappearing Dinosaur

## Read more Jigsaw Jones Mysteries by James Preller

*The Case from Outer Space*–New!

*The Case of the Smelly Sneaker*

*The Case of the Bicycle Bandit*

*The Case of the Glow-in-the-Dark Ghost*

*The Case of the Mummy Mystery*

*The Case of the Best Pet Ever*

*The Case of the Buried Treasure*

*The Case of the Disappearing Dinosaur*

*The Case of the Million-Dollar Mystery*

A JIGSAW JONES MYSTERY

# The Case of the Disappearing Dinosaur

by James Preller

illustrated by Jamie Smith

cover illustration by R. W. Alley

FEIWEL AND FRIENDS
New York

A Feiwel and Friends Book
An imprint of Macmillan Publishing Group, LLC
175 Fifth Avenue, New York, NY 10010

 Printed in the United States of America by LSC Communications, Harrisonburg, Virginia.



Library of Congress Cataloging-in-Publication Data is available.

ISBN 978-1-250-11088-6 (paperback) / ISBN 978-1-250-11087-9 (ebook)

Book design by Véronique Lefèvre Sweet
Illustrations by Jamie Smith

Feiwel and Friends logo designed by Filomena Tuosto

First Feiwel and Friends edition, 2017

Originally published by Scholastic in 2002

Art used with permission from Scholastic

1 3 5 7 9 10 8 6 4 2

mackids.com

*For Sierra and Sage*

# Contents

# Danika the Great

It was a perfect Saturday afternoon. Blue sky, no clouds, no worries. One of those days you'd like to slide into a Xerox machine and copy 365 times.

You could call it a year.

And every day would be Saturday.

Too bad I was stuck inside, sitting on Danika Starling's living room floor. I was doing a lot of nothing much and pretending to be happy about it. Suddenly, Danika swept into the room wearing a top hat and cape. She beamed while Mila and I politely applauded. Off to the side, Lucy Hiller frowned unhappily. "Nuh-uh," Lucy said. "Your entrance still needs something. It's got no style. No zip."

"What do you mean, no zip?" Danika complained. "I haven't even started my magic act yet."

"You're taking the stage, Danika," Lucy stated. "You're putting on a big show. You've got to grab the audience's attention right away."

"Lucy!" I groaned. "She's rehearsing for a birthday party. What do you expect? Flashing lights and stink bombs?"

"Jigsaw, you're a wonderful detective. But leave the magic act to us," Lucy commented. Suddenly, her eyes lit up. "I've got it! Danika, you need a snazzy opening. Something peppy and fun. With loud music. You know, big drums and electric guitars. And this time, I'll give you a snappy introduction."

Lucy gently pushed Danika out of the room. "Come in after I announce you," she instructed.

Danika did as she was told. Then Lucy, all curls and big eyes, turned to Mila and me. "Welcome, ladies and gentlemen!" she boomed. "It is time for our incredible magic show. Please put your hands together for . . . Danika the Great!"

At that instant, Lucy blasted music from WFLY 92—the station with "all the hits and none of the misses." *Boom, boom, boom.* Loud music rocked the walls. I plugged my fingers in my ears. Once again, Danika swept into the room, her cape flowing behind her. Lucy cut the music and clapped. "Fabulous! Fabulous! That's *much* better!" she exclaimed. "Don't you agree, Mila?"

Mila nodded happily. "I can't wait until the party tomorrow."

"I *am* waiting," I pointed out. "And I'm

getting bored, too. I thought we were going to play baseball."

"In a minute, Jigsaw," Mila shushed. "First, Danika needs an audience so she can practice her magic act."

"I've got a magic trick," I mumbled. "How about if *we* disappear?" I felt a sharp pain in my ribs. *Yeesh*. Mila sure had pointy elbows. I guessed baseball would have to wait.

"Did someone say *disappear*?" Lucy asked.

"Um, never mind," I said.

"That's our big trick, when we really do make something disappear!" Lucy winked at Danika. "But it's an extra-special trick. We're not showing you that one today."

Danika raised her hands to silence the chatter. She told us, "I'm not *only* a magician. I'm also a mind reader. But I'll need the help of the audience."

Danika explained that she would turn her

back. We could then take any coin—a penny, nickel, dime, or quarter—and give it to her assistant, Lucy. I fished a nickel from my pocket and kissed it good-bye. Lucy put it on the table. She placed a coffee cup over it.

"You can turn around now, Danika!" Lucy hollered.

Danika stared at the ceiling. She rubbed her eyes and strained under the effort. "Please," she hissed. "You must all *concentrate* on the coin. I will read your minds."

Danika haltingly murmured, "The answer is . . . a nickel."

"Again!" I demanded.

This time I handed Lucy a dime. Once more, Danika asked us to concentrate. Well, Mila must have thought about that dime pretty hard. Because all I was thinking was, *How did Danika pull off that trick?*

"Hmmmm," Danika said, biting her lip. "This is very difficult." She glanced at the cup and closed her eyes. "I see it now," she said.

"The answer is . . . a dime!"

# Lost and Found

Mila and I left for the park about fifteen minutes later. Actually, Lucy kicked us out. "We've still got a few more tricks to practice on our own," Lucy told us. "We don't want to reveal our amazing secrets."

Mila seemed disappointed. I slapped a baseball into my glove and pulled down my hat. "We are *outta* here," I blurted.

On the way to Lincoln Park, Mila said, "She's pretty good, don't you think, Jigsaw?"

"I'm not a big fan of magic," I confessed.

"I feel like it's cheating. Like everything is one big trick."

"Duh," Mila replied. "That's the whole idea, isn't it? How do you think Danika did that mind-reading act?"

"I was wondering about that," I said. "It must be a code or something. I figure that Lucy gives her a secret signal."

"Or maybe she really *can* read minds," Mila suggested.

"Maybe cats can ride pogo sticks," I replied. "But I kind of doubt it. That mind-reading act is as fake as a rubber chicken that lays scrambled eggs. I only wish I could figure out how Danika does it."

We spent the next half hour catching flies on the soggy grass. No, not the flies with wings and creepy suction feet. I'm a kid, not

a frog. I was using my baseball glove—not a long, sticky tongue.

I threw the baseball in a high, long arc to Mila. She drifted back and caught it easily. Mila is a good ballplayer. She is also my partner. We're detectives. For a dollar a day, we make problems go away. We've found missing hamsters and stolen bicycles,

runaway dogs and brownie bandits. But today we were catching baseballs, not bad guys.

That is, until Joey Pignattano and Ralphie Jordan came running over. “We’ve been searching all over for you guys,” Joey wheezed.

“You should have looked here first,” I said. “It would have saved you time.”

“Huh?”

“Ignore him, Joey,” Mila said. “What’s up?”

Joey pulled a coin purse from his jeans pocket. The purse was made of red satin, with a little silver clip on the top.

“Go ahead, Joey. Show ’em,” Ralphie urged.

So Joey showed us. He opened the purse—and all I saw was green. Lots of green. The color of money.

Mila whistled softly. “Where did you get this?”

"We found it on the way to the candy store," Joey said excitedly. "It was on the ground. Just sitting there. Doing nothing."

I held out my hand. "May I?"

I emptied the purse onto the ground. Out spilled a red lipstick, a few rubber bands, thirty-seven cents in change, a scrap of paper, two ticket stubs, and a gang of dead presidents. That is, *pictures* of dead presidents. Two portraits of Andrew Jackson, three of Abraham Lincoln, and eight George Washingtons. In other words, sixty-three dollars.

I eyed Joey closely. "What do you plan on doing with this money?"

"We've got to find the owner," Joey said, eyes unblinking. "That's why I came to you."

"Good answer, Joey. But you know our rates. We get a dollar a day," I reminded him.

Joey frowned. "I'm not made of money, Jigsaw. Besides, I just spent my whole allowance on candy."

"There will probably be a reward when we return it," Ralphie said. "Maybe you could split it with us."

We shook hands and called it a deal. Baseball would have to wait. Because Joey Pignattano had just thrown us a fat pitch right over the plate. We had to take a swing at it.

# Lining Up the Clues

Mila looked over the contents of the purse. She folded the money neatly and placed it back inside the purse. She returned the rubber bands, lipstick, and loose change, then snapped the purse shut.

"What about the rest?" Joey wondered.

Mila didn't answer. Instead, she read the piece of paper. It was a list, written in a sloppy scrawl.

Wrapping Paper
Tape
Card
Candles
Pick up
CAKE!!!

"Is that a clue?" Ralphie asked.

"It's a shopping list," Mila replied. *"And a clue."*

"So is this." I pointed at the blue ticket stub. "Too bad it's been ripped in half. I'm not sure I can read all of the words."

Joey peered over my shoulder. "What's a TER PAN?"

"The play *Peter Pan* has been showing this week at the Steamer Ten Theater," I answered. "I know because my sister Hillary's in it. She plays one of the Lost Boys. Go figure. Anyway, it's all she's been talking about for weeks."

Mila pulled on her long black hair. "March eleventh–that's yesterday."

"But how's all this going to help us find the lady who lost the purse?" Joey asked.

"Mysteries are like jigsaw puzzles," I told Joey. "You keep looking at the pieces until they fit together. That's how you solve the case. For example, you said it was a *lady's* purse. We don't know that for sure. Not all women carry purses and wear lipstick. And not all people who carry purses are women. We have to keep our minds open."

"I don't think many kids carry around that kind of cash," Ralphie noted.

Holding the purse in her hand, Mila concluded, "The person who lost this purse probably went to see *Peter Pan* last night." She studied the ticket stub once more. Puzzled, she read aloud, "I-N-E-E ONLY?"

"It could be the row," Joey suggested. "Like you were only allowed to sit IN row EE."

Before I could reply to that, a shout startled me. "HEY, YOU RATS! GIVE ME BACK MY MOTHER'S MONEY!"

Bobby Solofsky jumped off his bicycle, letting it crash to the ground. "I'll take that purse," he demanded. "It belongs to my mom." Bobby snatched at the purse.

"Not so fast, cowboy," I said, stepping between Bobby and the purse. "You'll have to prove it first."

The first time I met Bobby Solofsky, I caught him trying to steal Cheez Doodles from my lunch box. That was way back in preschool. But some things never change. Like my dad says, "A zebra can't change his stripes."

And Bobby Solofsky couldn't change his ways. He was as straight as a plate of soggy spaghetti.

And twice as slippery.

# Something Fishy

"Prove it?!" Bobby repeated, his voice rising in disbelief. "PROVE IT?!"

The tips of his ears turned red with anger. "Prove it" was not what Bobby wanted to hear. Still, looking at the four of us standing across from him, Bobby saw there would be no other way. "Okay. I *will* prove it," he finally snapped back.

"Good," I answered. "What was in the purse?"

"Money. Gobs of it," Bobby replied. "My

mom's money—and I want it back, every stinking penny."

I let out a slow, sleepy yawn. Ho-hum. "Strike one. Anybody could have guessed that, Solofsky. What *else* was in the purse?"

A smile visited Bobby's face. It looked lost there, like a tourist who'd taken the wrong bus. Smiles didn't usually find their way to Bobby's face. Smirks and sneers, yes. Smiles? Nope, not often.

I repeated the question to Solofsky.

He paused, thinking it over. "Oh, yeah, I remember," Bobby said. "Tickets! My mom and me went to see *Peter Pan* last night."

There it was, that same fishy smile swimming across his face. I didn't like the look of it. "You?" I exclaimed. *"Peter Pan?!"*

Bobby folded his arms across a New York Yankees T-shirt. "Yeah, I always liked Twinkle Bell."

"*Tinker* Bell," Mila corrected.

"Whatever," Solofsky snorted. "Just hand over the green stuff."

"Sorry, Solofsky. I can't do that," I replied. "There's something fishy about your story."

"What do fish have to do with this?" Bobby protested.

"Both smell," I replied.

I turned to Joey. "Who *else* knows about this purse you found?"

"Nobody," Joey answered. He bit his lip. "Except, er, maybe we showed Mike Radcliff."

"And Eddie Becker," Ralphie added. "And Geetha Nair and Kim Lewis and . . ."

I raised my hand. "Hold on. Is there anyone you *didn't* tell?"

Ralphie pointed at Bobby. "Yeah . . . him!"

I knew that Mike Radcliff was Bobby Solofsky's best friend. So I asked, "Did you show Mike and the others what was inside the purse?"

Joey nodded and sheepishly bleated, "Yes. Did I mess up?"

"Mike Radcliff is Bobby's neighbor," I pointed out. "He could have easily told Bobby about the purse–and what was inside it."

"So what?!" Bobby protested. A spray of spit spewed from his mouth. Ugh. If I needed a shower, I would have taken one at home.

"Mike is my friend," Bobby said. "Besides,

it wasn't a secret. So what if he *did* tell me about the purse. Mike's a good guy. Obviously, you rats wanted to keep the money for yourselves."

"Save your breath, Solofsky. You're wasting air," I said. "This is *not* your mom's purse—and you never went to see *Peter Pan* last night."

"How would you know?" Bobby challenged.

"I swung an imaginary baseball bat in my hands. 'It's Tinker Bell, not Twinkle Bell. That's strike two."

"Anybody could make a little mistake," Bobby said.

I shrugged. "Maybe yes, maybe no. Second, you said you saw the play last night. But look at this ripped ticket. It says 'I-N-E-E.' The first three letters are missing: M, A, and T. This ticket is for the MATINEE ONLY."

NY
NEW YORK
YANKEES

Bobby stared blankly. I could tell I'd reached the outer limits of his vocabulary.

"A matinee is an *afternoon* show," Mila explained. "You said you went last night. You lied, Solofsky."

I swung the imaginary bat once again. "Strike three, Bobby. You just whiffed with the bases loaded."

Solofsky scratched his head, muttering to himself. He was trying to think of a clever reply. It looked like it put a strain on his brain. Finally, Bobby pointed at me and cried, "I'll get you back for this, Jigsaw Jones. Sooner or later, I'll make you pay."

We watched him ride off in silence. Then Ralphie slapped me on the back. "Great work, Jigsaw!"

Joey still seemed troubled. "Then *whose* purse is it?"

"This shopping list might give us the answer," Mila said. "Follow me, guys! I've got an idea."

# How the Cookie Crumbles

Mila led us to a tidy row of stores on Waverly Avenue. We stopped about ten feet from Huck's Hardware. Joey pointed to the ground beside a row of hedges. "We found the purse right there," he told her.

I knelt down with my handy-dandy magnifying glass. The dirt was still wet from last night's rain. When I stood up, my knees were muddy.

Mom wasn't going to like that. But, hey, what are knees for, anyway?

"It rained hard last night," Mila noted. "But the satin purse was pretty dry. No bad water stains. The owner must have dropped the purse this morning."

"Makes sense to me," I agreed. "Let me look at that list again."

Ralphie read over my shoulder. He noted, "I bet one of these stores sells tape, cards, candles, and wrapping paper."

"But what about the cake?" I asked. "That's the important item on this list. Look at the writing. All capital letters. Three exclamation points. Then look at the other items on the list. Candles, card, wrapping paper, tape. I'd bet my baseball cap it's somebody's birthday."

"Where can you get a cake around here?" Mila asked.

Joey and Ralphie grinned happily. "Grandma's Bakery!" they chimed.

*Ching, ching*. Bells jingle-jangled when we opened the front door. Grandma's Bakery was cool and airy and it smelled like a slice of heaven. Two teenage girls stood behind a glass counter filled with pastries. The tall girl smiled, flashing big white teeth. The other girl was short and grim. She looked like she'd just swallowed a sourball. I noticed that her hair was a spiky mess. It was possibly the worst haircut I'd ever seen—and I'd seen a few in my time. Sometimes on top of my own head.

I asked the tall girl if anyone had picked up a birthday cake this morning.

"Why should we tell you?" the Bad-Haircut-Girl sniped.

"I'm working on a case," I explained. "I'm a detective." I handed her a business card.

The Bad-Haircut-Girl sneered, "Yeah, right. You don't look like detectives to me."

"Oh, just ignore Brenda," the tall girl remarked. She pulled out a thick black book filled with the day's receipts. "We keep track of our special orders," she informed us, leafing through the pages.

"Let's see . . . a man came in and picked up two chocolate cream pies. Then an older woman, Mrs. Alessi, left with two dozen strawberry cupcakes."

"Yum," Joey moaned. "I love strawberry cupcakes."

"Anyone else?" I prodded.

"Hmmmm," the tall girl mused. "Yes, yes, here it is. Mrs. Maloney bought a birthday cake for her son Charlie. I remember the name because I did the lettering myself."

"Charlie Maloney!" Mila exclaimed. "That's Bigs! Of course. His birthday party is tomorrow afternoon. That ties in with the note we found in the purse! His mom must

have dropped it this morning when she picked up the cake."

I thanked the nice girl behind the counter, grunted at the mean one, and copied down the phone number from the receipt. Then I asked if I could borrow one of their phones. "It's business," I explained.

Fifteen minutes later, Mrs. Maloney rushed into the store. She had a toddler at her feet and another one in her arms. What a racket. Carrying around a screaming police siren might have been quieter. And drier. The kids looked like identical twins. Probably because they were. I'd met them before at Bigs Maloney's house. Larry and Harry.

Poor Mrs. Maloney looked about as calm as a Siamese cat at a dog show. She was just the type to drop a purse and not notice.

"Jigsaw!" she exclaimed when she saw us. "Thank you so much for calling. What an honest young man!"

"Don't thank me," I said. "It was these two.

You know Joey Pignattano and Ralphie Jordan. They're the heroes who found your purse."

Mrs. Maloney smiled at them. Suddenly, she noticed Mila for the first time. "Oh, hello, Mila! I guess we'll be seeing you at the party tomorrow, too?"

Mila smiled. "Yep, we'll all be there. Bigs invited everyone from Ms. Gleason's class—even the girls."

Just then, one of the twins sprang a leak or something. A puddle formed on the floor. On cue, the twin in Mrs. Maloney's arms started to wail. "Wah-wah-wah-waaaaaaaaaaah!"

"Oh, for crying out loud," groaned Mrs. Maloney. "What a day. Still, I'm so grateful to you children. How can I *possibly* thank you?"

Joey offered a suggestion.

And like most of Joey's ideas, it involved food.

Two minutes later, Mrs. Maloney drove off in her car. Mila and I made sure the coin purse was safely tucked into her pocketbook.

Joey, Ralphie, Mila, and I went outside and

sat under an old willow tree. The grass was nice and dry beneath it. Each of us bit into our very own black-and-white cookie.

"Awesome!" Joey exclaimed.

And he was right.

It was our reward. Thanks to Mrs. Maloney.

We all chewed happily. In silence. Enjoying every bite. Because that's the way the black-and-white cookie crumbles.

It pays to be honest. And that's something that guys like Bobby Solofsky would never understand. Happily eating under the tree, I thought my detective work was done for the weekend. But I didn't realize that another case awaited us. It involved a dinosaur. A birthday party. And a magic trick that went very, very wrong.

# Go, Rags, Go!

Mila and I have been sending secret messages to each other since dinosaurs ruled the earth. Okay, maybe not *that* long. But it has been a while. Codes are the best way for detectives to talk to each other—and it's fun, too. Besides, like my favorite baseball team, the New York Mets, we needed the practice.

After doing the dishes that night, I went into my bedroom with my trusty dog, Rags. I figure Rags liked to think that he was helping on a case in some way. Or maybe he just liked sleeping on my soft, thick rug.

I decided to try an IPPY Code. It was simple. All you had to do was add the letters IP after every consonant in each word. So the word DOG becomes DIPOGIP and BIGS becomes BIPIGIPSIP.

I wrote:

I BIPOUGIPHIPTIP BIPIGIPSIP
A DIPINIPOSIPAURIP PIPUZIPZIPLIPE.
WIPHIPATIP DIPIDIP YIPOU GIPETIP
HIPIMIP?

Now no one could read it. Except for Mila. She already knew about IPPY codes. To decode it, all Mila had to do was cross out all the IP letters.

I called Mila on the phone. "Don't talk," I warned. "Enemies may be listening. Just stand by your front door, wave a doggy snack, and call Rags. Got it?"

Mila coughed three times. That was our signal. She understood. I hung up the phone and taped the message inside Rags's collar. "Okay, Ragsy," I said. "Time to do your stuff."

Mila lived down the block–and Rags knew the way by heart. Or, I guess, by nose. I opened the front door and whispered to Rags, "Go, boy. Find Mila."

Rags looked at me, wondering why I wasn't coming with him. Why was he standing outside? Why was his nose always wet and cold?

"Rags! *Raaaaags!* I've got a treat for you!" Mila's voice threaded through the distance.

Rags's keen ears lifted. He suddenly understood the meaning of life. It was all about food, glorious food! Off he raced,

chasing the promise of doggy snacks, hungry as a sumo wrestler at a free buffet.

Good old Rags. Sure, maybe Shaggy had Scooby-Doo. But I had my own flea-bitten hairball to help with detective work.

Rags. A detective's best friend.

# Meet Buster

Mila, Ralphie, Joey, and I piled into our minivan. We were late for Bigs Maloney's birthday party. Joey kept licking his lips and whispering, *"I want cake, I want cake."*

"Shhh, Joey," Mila hushed. "There's more to a party than eating cake."

"I know," Joey said. "But I can't stop thinking about cake ever since we went to Grandma's Bakery yesterday."

"Buckle up," my dad urged. "Let's get a move on. I've got to get back to take Daniel and Nicholas to soccer practice. Then I've got to drive Hillary to the Steamer Ten Theater." He sighed. "I feel like I spend half my life shuttling you kids to practices and dentist appointments and birthday parties. One of these days I'm going to trade in this minivan and get myself a little red sports car."

I'd heard that speech a million times before. Except my dad usually described the goggles and long white scarf he'd wear. But that's grown-ups for you. They're always complaining about something, usually us kids. It's like they forget they used to be short once, too.

Go figure.

At the front door of the Maloneys' house, we heard crying and screaming and the yip-yip-yapping of a small puppy. "I didn't know Bigs had a dog," Mila said.

The door swung open and a small brown dog leaped at our throats. *Yip-yip-yip* it yapped, scratching at Ralphie's

pant leg. "Down, Buster, down, boy!" Bigs commanded.

Meanwhile Buster, the dog, kept bouncing up and down like a fluffy basketball. Licking, yipping, yapping.

"Somebody gave that dog too much coffee," Ralphie joked.

"He's adorable!" Mila gushed. She bent down to pet the puppy, only to get licked like a lollipop. "I've been slimed," Mila moaned.

Bigs introduced us. "This is Buster. We just got him yesterday. He's my birthday present."

Mrs. Maloney appeared behind Bigs. As usual, she had a baby in her arms. The other twin toddled near her feet, gurgling and laughing at Buster's antics. "Yes, a new dog," Mrs. Maloney said, looking tired and frazzled. "We didn't think life was crazy enough already."

I laughed. "I've got three brothers and a sister . . . *and* a big dog," I told her. "Our house gets pretty noisy sometimes. My dad calls it a joyful racket. Except I'm not sure he always thinks it's so joyful."

"Five kids! That *does* sound like a racket," Mrs. Maloney said. With a weary grunt, she heaved a baby from one arm to the other. "You've already met the twins. This is Larry. And that's Harry," she added, eyes toward the ground. "He's the one sucking on Jigsaw's sneakers."

Yeesh. What a party. First dog slime, then baby slobber, and we hadn't even gotten

past the front door. "Okay, Larry. No more eating my sneakie-weakies," I cooed.

"No, Jigsaw. *That's* Larry," Mila said, pointing at the baby in Mrs. Maloney's arms. "The one washing your shoes with drool is Harry."

That's the problem with twins. They'd be okay, I guess, except they look alike. "Do *you* ever get them mixed up?" I asked Mrs. Maloney.

"I hope not!" Mrs. Maloney laughed. "Actually, there's an easy way to tell the difference. Larry has a freckle on his nose. Harry doesn't. But please, come on in. You can put your presents on the table. Everyone is out in the backyard. Mr. Maloney is getting ready to begin the water-balloon toss as we speak."

"Great!" We raced through the house and into the backyard, screaming at the top of our lungs.

# The Magic Show

I always said that Bigs Maloney was built like a soda machine. But Bigs was nothing compared to his father. Mr. Maloney looked like the truck that *delivered* the soda machines. He was bigger than big. He was gigantic.

Mr. Maloney filled water balloons from a garden hose. A group of kids swarmed around him, like gnats on a gorilla. "What does your father do for a living?" I whispered to Bigs. "Climb the Empire State Building and swat down planes?"

Bigs laughed. "No, Jigsaw. That's King Kong."

"So sue me," I answered with a shrug. "Maybe I got them confused."

"Actually, I'm a florist," Mr. Maloney's deep voice answered.

"A florist," I murmured. "You look like you could play linebacker for the Chicago Bears."

Mr. Maloney laughed, like he'd heard that kind of comment before. "I played a little ball back in my day," he replied. "But now I work with flowers mostly. Anyway, that's about it for these water balloons. Let the games begin!"

For the next half hour, we played water-balloon toss, ran egg-on-a-spoon relay races, and even had a giant tug-of-war. All the kids from Ms. Gleason's class were there. Bigs Maloney's twin brothers, Harry and Larry, were crawling all over the place. I saw them almost get stepped on about twelve times.

Even Buster got into the action, chewing on the garden hose.

"He chews on *everything*," Mr. Maloney said. "Typical Labrador. If you don't keep an eye on them, they'll chew your house to pieces."

Lucy Hiller suddenly cupped her hands around her mouth and yelled. "Ladies and gentlemen, boys and girls! Danika the Great will now amaze you with her magical

talents. Please follow me into the basement. Our show is about to begin!"

We crammed into the basement.

I got bumped from behind. I turned and saw Bobby Solofsky.

"Whoops," he said. "My elbow must have slipped."

We exchanged dirty looks and sat down.

Lucy stood behind a desk. A cloth covered it and draped to the floor. Everyone cheered when Danika took the stage to the *thump-thump-wacka-wacka-THUMP* of loud music.

I have to admit it. Danika did a great job. She performed the mind-reading trick with the cup again. But this time I figured it out. I noticed that Lucy changed the direction of the cup's handle each time she covered a new coin. It was a secret signal, I realized. Like a code. If the handle pointed to Danika's left, it was a penny. If it faced away from Danika, then it was a nickel. To the right, a dime. And facing Danika meant a quarter. Like this:

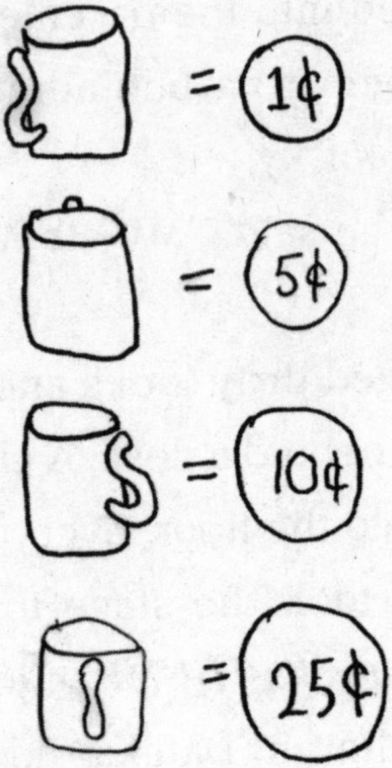

= 1¢

= 5¢

= 10¢

= 25¢

I had to cheer. They sure had everyone else fooled.

Danika did some card tricks. Next she took a clear plastic cup of water and put a piece of paper on it. Then she turned it upside down—and the water didn't spill out!

Mila whispered, "My father taught me that one. It's done with a little hole near the

bottom of the glass. Danika covers the hole with her finger and the water can't fall out."

I didn't argue with her.

"I will now levitate a human being," Danika said.

"What's *levitate*?" Joey asked.

"And what's a human *bean*?" Stringbean Noonan wondered.

Danika rubbed her eyes, like she felt a headache coming on. "I mean, I'll make my assistant, Lucy, float in midair," Danika explained.

Danika stood in front of the table. She asked Lucy to lie on the floor on her back. Danika took a large sheet and covered Lucy. It wasn't easy, because Harry (or was it Larry?) kept getting in the way. Meanwhile, Buster sniffed underneath the table. Danika waved a wand and said some magical mumbo-jumbo.

We all gasped when Lucy and the sheet rose about a foot into the air.

*"Presto-finito,"* Danika cried out.

Lucy slowly lowered to the floor.

The room went wild with cheers and applause.

"That's easy," Bobby Solofsky barked. "Lucy turned and got on her stomach right when Danika covered her with the sheet. She didn't float in the air. Lucy did a push-up!"

Danika stared angrily at Bobby. Then she said, "For my final trick, I will make something disappear." She glanced around the room and saw Bigs Maloney's dinosaur display. She took a plastic stegosaurus and held it up for all to see. Danika slowly sat behind the table. "And now," she whispered, pausing for effect, "my greatest trick of all. . . ."

# Gone!

I leaned forward and watched closely. I wanted to figure out another one of Danika's tricks. From her seat behind the table, Danika took a paper napkin and tried to wrap it around the dinosaur. But the paper kept ripping.

"Darn, this one is too big," Danika said. Lucy handed her a smaller stuffed dinosaur.

"Wait!" Bigs cried. "That's Spike, my favorite dinosaur. Don't make *him* disappear!"

Danika smiled. "Don't worry, Bigs. I'll make Spike reappear again."

"Promise?"

"I promise," Danika replied.

This time, Danika had no problem covering it with a napkin. She held it up for all to see. A puzzled look crossed her face, and she glanced under the table. "Hello, down there," she cooed. Danika smiled. "One of the babies is chewing on my shoe," she told us with a laugh.

Suddenly, *whap, whap*, Danika slapped the paper napkin and the dinosaur on the table twice. She raised her hand to slap it down a third time . . . *thud*. The napkin flattened on the table.

The dinosaur was gone!

"Now, to make it reappear . . ." Danika announced. I noticed one of her shoulders droop slightly, like maybe she was reaching under the table for something. "Er, um, just a second," Danika mumbled.

Lucy saw that Danika was in trouble and turned on the music again. *Boom-boom, whacka-boom,* the speakers throbbed. A few more moments crawled by. Danika's face turned red. "I'm having a little problem," she admitted.

"Where's Spike?" Bigs demanded.

"He's, um . . ." Danika bent over to look

underneath the table. Danika sat back up. “Spike has, er, disappeared.”

“We already know that,” Bobby Solofsky sneered.

“Yeah, bring him back,” Bigs demanded.

“You don’t get it, Bigs,” Danika confessed. “Spike has *really* disappeared.”

A wave of nervous laughter rolled through the room. Was this part of the act?

"What a rotten trick!" scowled Solofsky.

I glanced at Mila, who nodded toward Bigs. He seemed upset. I saw his lower lip tremble. "It's not funny," Bigs charged. "That's my favorite dinosaur, and you promised you'd bring him back."

Danika's face turned from red to chalk white. "I'm not *trying* to be funny," she said. "Somebody, somehow, must have stolen Spike. I'm telling you, Bigs, I don't have your dinosaur!"

## Chapter 10

# The Scene of the Crime

Everyone was stunned. Voices and shouts filled the room. I stood and pointed at Danika, "Don't touch a thing, Danika. No one leaves this room," I commanded.

Mila and I walked up to Danika. Lucy stood by her side. "Are you telling the truth?" I whispered.

Danika's eyes widened. She looked directly into mine. "Yes, Jigsaw. Help me, please. I honestly don't know what happened to the dinosaur."

"We get a dollar a day," I said.

"In advance," Mila added.

Danika nodded. "Sure, sure, anything. Just get me out of this mess." She glanced toward Bigs, then handed me a dollar bill. It disappeared into my pocket. Neat trick, huh?

"I'll interview the witnesses," Mila said.

I nodded. "Start with Solofsky. Whenever there's trouble, he's usually in the middle of it. Here, take my journal. But first, let me do one thing." I turned to a clean page and wrote:

CASE: The Disappearing Dinosaur
CLIENT: Danika Starling

Mila got everyone to stay seated. One by one, she asked them questions. Meanwhile, I talked to Danika and Lucy. "You were looking under the table," I said. "Are you sure the dinosaur isn't there?"

"See for yourself," Danika answered. We lifted up the tablecloth. There was an empty shoe box under the desk, padded with a

soft cloth, and not much else. Besides Buster, of course, who was busily chewing on a desk leg.

"Tell me exactly how this trick was supposed to work," I asked Danika.

"No way!" Lucy protested. "A magician never reveals her secrets."

I crossed my arms. "Get real, Lucy," I said. "We have to solve this mystery. I need to know all the facts."

Lucy locked eyes with Danika. Together, in silence, they seemed to decide something. "It's like this . . ." Danika began.

The trick was simple, actually. It began when Danika sat behind the desk. When she folded the napkin over the dinosaur, Danika made sure to leave the bottom uncovered. Then she let the dinosaur slip into her lap. The trick was that the paper napkin still kept the shape of the dinosaur. No one noticed that it was missing.

"When you slapped it against the table, it made a noise, even though the napkin was empty," I noted.

Danika reached under and, *whap, whap,* knocked against the bottom of the table. She said, "The third time, I just flattened the napkin."

"Got it," I said. "So you're saying the dinosaur should still be on your lap?"

Lucy shook her head. "No, Danika is *supposed* to take it and stuff it into the box."

"I DID stuff it into the box," Danika claimed. "That's what's so weird."

I looked down at Buster, still chewing at the table. I lifted my baseball cap and scratched the back of my neck. "Did you eat it, Buster?" I asked.

Buster didn't answer.

"Great," I mumbled. "What every detective loves. We've got one witness. But he isn't talking."

# A Surprise Ending

Mila joined us. "No one has much to say," she told me. "And Bobby never left his seat. Some kids said they saw movement under the table. But that was probably just Larry. Remember, he was under there for a while."

"Larry?" I asked. "Or Harry?"

"Same thing," Mila replied. "Isn't it?"

I guessed she was right.

"Jigsaw thinks maybe Buster ate it," Danika told Mila.

Mila looked at the ground. She frowned. "Buster is a chewer," she said, "not a swallower. There would be bits of cloth and stuffing on the ground, don't you think?"

I did think.

And Mila was probably right.

We talked over the case. Mila again asked Danika, "You say you stuffed it into the box? Are you sure?"

"I told you three times now," Danika said. "I reached down, felt the cloth, and stuffed it in there."

"But you had to do it quickly," I said. "That's part of the trick, right?"

Danika nodded. "Yeah, it's not like I have all day."

*Whoops! Crash!* One of the babies, Harry or Larry, knocked over a lamp. The other one squatted in the doorway. He seemed sort of . . . *uncomfortable*. "Hey, Bigs," I called. "Better get one of your parents. I think maybe your brother just did his business, if you know what I mean."

Bigs walked over to his little brother. He bent down and sniffed. "I don't think so, Jigsaw. He doesn't smell too funky."

"Wait a minute," I said. "Is he the one who was playing under the table?"

Bigs shrugged.

Mila shrugged.

Danika shrugged.

Twins. Who can tell the difference?

"What are you thinking, Jigsaw?" Mila asked.

I felt the fabric in the box on the floor. It was denim. Like the kind used to make jeans and overalls.

"How does he feel around the, er, behind area?" I asked Bigs.

"Nuh-uh," Bigs said, waving his hands. "Not my job. I'm not touching it."

I gulped. As a rule, I tried to stay far away from any baby's bottom. It wasn't a place I wanted to be. But I suddenly had a crazy hunch. And a mystery was a mystery. It was my job to get to the bottom of it. Even if the bottom of it was attached to a baby's actual bottom.

Sigh.

"Come here, little guy," I cooed. I noticed a freckle on the end of his nose. Must be Larry. "Anybody know how to get these overalls off?" I asked, tugging on the straps.

"Um, I don't think that's such a good idea," Bigs advised.

"It's a risk we'll have to take," I said.

"Here, let me help you," Mila said. She unsnapped a snap, unbuckled the buckles, undid the straps, and the top half of Larry's overalls sagged to the ground. There in the back of his pants, right next to his tush, was Bigs Maloney's missing dinosaur.

"Spike!" Bigs exclaimed. "How'd you get in there?"

Danika looked at me in surprise.

Larry seemed pretty surprised himself, like he'd just discovered some kind of amazing new talent. *Abracadabra!* Dinosaurs appeared out of his behind!

"Larry was under the table," I explained. "You must have stuffed the dinosaur into his overalls by mistake."

We all got a good laugh out of that one.

Suddenly, the lights dimmed. A glow came from the top of the stairs. *Creak, creak*. Heavy footfalls made the stairs groan. It was

Mr. and Mrs. Maloney, carrying a cake with candles. The cake from Grandma's Bakery, from a case we solved only yesterday.

We sang to Bigs,

> *"Happy Birthday to you,*
> *Happy Birthday to you,*
> *You look like a monkey,*
> *And you act like one, too!"*

And that was the end of that. Another case solved. It didn't take magic. Just a spike-tailed dinosaur that didn't feel too comfortable in somebody's overalls. I guess it all started with a good guy named Joey Pignattano—an honest guy who found some money. All he wanted to do was the right thing.

Mila suddenly burst out laughing. "What's so funny?" I asked.

"Oh, I was just thinking about the look on little Larry's face when we found that dinosaur in his pants. He was stunned. It's

Happy Birthday
Charlie

like he was sort of *proud*, you know. Like he did it all by himself!"

"Well, I've heard of the goose that laid golden eggs," I said. "Maybe Larry thinks he's the baby who lays plush dinosaurs!"

"Or was that Harry?" asked Danika.

"What*ever*!" Mila and I chimed back.

**Don't miss this special sneak peek at a brand-new, never-before-published JIGSAW JONES MYSTERY:**

# The Case from Outer Space

**"Highly recommended."**—***School Library Journal***

When **Joey** and **Danika** find a mysterious note tucked inside a book, all signs point to a visitor from outer space. Yikes! Can Jigsaw solve this case, when the clues are out of this world?

# A Knock on the Door

Call me Jones.

Jigsaw Jones, private eye.

I solve mysteries. For a dollar a day, I make problems go away. I've found stolen bicycles, lost jewelry, and missing parakeets. I've even tangled with dancing ghosts and haunted scarecrows.

Mysteries can happen anywhere, at any time. One thing I've learned in this business is that anyone is a suspect. That includes friends, family, and a little green man from outer space.

Go figure.

It was a lazy Sunday morning. Outside my window, it looked like a nice spring day. The sky was blue with wispy clouds that looked like they had been painted by an artist. A swell day for a ball game. Or a mystery. Maybe both if I got lucky.

I was standing at my dining room table, staring at a 500-piece jigsaw puzzle. It was supposed to be a picture of our solar system. The sun and eight planets. But right now it was a mess. Scattered pieces lay everywhere. I scratched my head and munched on a blueberry Pop-Tart. Not too hot, not too cold. *Just right.* As a cook, I'm pretty good with a toaster. I began working on the border, grouping all the pieces that had a flat edge. Sooner or later, I'd work my way through the planets. The rust red of Mars. The rings of Saturn. And the green tint of Neptune. I've never met a puzzle I couldn't

solve. That's because I know the secret. The simple trick? Don't give up.

Don't ever give up.

My dog, Rags, leaped at the door. He barked and barked. A minute later, the doorbell rang. *Ding-a-ling, ding-dong.* That's the thing about Rags. He's faster than a doorbell. People have been coming to our house all his life. But for my dog, it's always the most exciting thing that ever happened.

Every single time.

"Get the door, Worm," my brother Billy said. He was sprawled on the couch, reading a book. Teenagers, yeesh.

"Why me?" I complained.

"Because I'm not doing it."

Billy kept reading.

Rags kept barking.

And the doorbell kept ringing.

Somebody was in a hurry.

I opened the door. Joey Pignattano and

Danika Starling were standing on my stoop. We were in the same class together, room 201, with Ms. Gleason.

"Hey, Jigsaw!" Danika waved. She bounced on her toes. The bright beads in her hair clicked and clacked.

"Boy, am I glad to see you!" Joey exclaimed. He burst into the room. "Got any water?"

“I would invite you inside, Joey,” I said, “but you beat me to it.”

Danika smiled.

“I ate half a bag of Jolly Ranchers this morning,” Joey announced. “Now my tongue feels super weird!”

“That’s not good for your teeth,” I said.

Joey looked worried. "My tongue isn't good for my teeth? Are you sure? They both live inside my mouth."

"Never mind," I said.

"Pipe down, guys!" Billy complained. "I'm reading here."

"Come into the kitchen," I told Joey and Danika. "We'll get fewer complaints. Besides, I've got grape juice. It's on the house."

"On the house?" Joey asked. "Is it safe?"

I blinked. "What?"

"You keep grape juice on your roof?" Joey asked.

Danika gave Joey a friendly shove. "Jigsaw said 'on the house.' He means it's free, Joey," she said, laughing.

Joey pushed back his glasses with an index finger. "Free? In that case, I'll take a big glass."

# One Small Problem

I poured three glasses of grape juice.

"Got any snacks?" Joey asked. "Cookies? Chips? Corn dogs? Crackers?"

"Corn dogs?" I repeated. "Seriously?"

"Oh, they are delicious," Joey said. "I ate six yesterday. Or was that last week? I forget."

Danika shook her head and giggled. Joey always made her laugh.

I set out a bowl of chips.

Joey pounced like a football player on a

fumble. He was a skinny guy, but he ate like a rhinoceros.

"So what's up?" I asked.

"We found a note," Danika began.

"Aliens are coming," Joey interrupted. He chomped on a fistful of potato chips.

I waited for Joey to stop chewing. It took a while. *Hum-dee-dum, dee-dum-dum.* I finally asked, "What do you mean, aliens?"

"Aliens, Jigsaw!" he exclaimed. "Little green men from Mars–from the stars–from outer space!"

Thank you for reading this **FEIWEL AND FRIENDS** book.

The Friends who made

# The Case of the Disappearing Dinosaur

possible are:

**Jean Feiwel,** Publisher

**Liz Szabla,** Asociate Publisher

**Rich Deas,** Senior Creative Director

**Holly West,** Editor

**Alexei Esikoff,** Senior Managing Editor

**Raymond Ernesto Colón,** Senior Production Manager

**Anna Roberto,** Editor

**Christine Barcellona,** Editor

**Kat Brzozowski,** Editor

**Emily Settle,** Administrative Assistant

**Anna Poon,** Assistant Editor

Follow us on Facebook or visit us online at mackids.com.

**OUR BOOKS ARE FRIENDS FOR LIFE.**